1895

Night-Night!

Seven going-to-bed stories
One wonderful story for every
night of the week

Morris Lurie

To John Bryson
a favourite child,
except for 'The Talking Bow Tie',
which belongs to Rachel,
and 'The Frog Who Would Sing For The King',
which is for Ben.
Thank you.

Illustrated by Alison Lester

Melbourne
Oxford University Press
Auckland New York

OXFORD UNIVERSITY PRESS

Oxford New York Toronto
Delhi Bombay Calcutta Madras Karachi
Kuala Lumpur Singapore Hong Kong Tokyo
Nairobi Dar es Salaam Cape Town
Melbourne Auckland
and associates in
Beirut Berlin Ibadan Nicosia

© Text Morris Lurie 1986
© Illustrations Alison Lester 1986
First published 1986

This book is copyright. Apart from any fair
dealing for the purposes of private study,
research, criticism or review as permitted under
the Copyright Act, no part may be reproduced,
stored in a retrieval system, or transmitted, in
any form or by any means, electronic, mechanical,
photocopying, recording, or otherwise without
prior written permission. Inquiries should be made
to Oxford University Press.

National Library of Australia
Cataloguing-in-Publication data:

Lurie, Morris.
    Night-night!: seven going-to-bed stories.

    ISBN 0 19 554739 X.

    1. Children's stories, Australian. I. Lester, Alison.
    II. Title.

A823'.3

Designed by Steven Dunbar
Etchings processed by Kevin Parratt at Field Gallery, South Melbourne
Typeset in 16 point Baskerville No. 2 by Bookset, Melbourne
Printed in Australia by Impact Printing, Melbourne
Published by Oxford University Press, 7 Bowen Crescent, Melbourne
OXFORD is a trademark of Oxford University Press

Contents

The Dragon Who Had Hiccups 5

The Talking Bow Tie 17

The Frog Who Would Sing For The King 25

Tiny Timothy 35

Elephant On The Doorstep 45

Rosie On The Swing 55

The Little Girl Who Did Not Believe
In Witches 63

The Dragon Who Had Hiccups

There was once a dragon who had hiccups.

'I don't know where they came from, hic,' said the dragon sadly. 'But here they are.'

'Boo!' cried his brother Nigel, leaping out suddenly from behind a door.

The dragon who had hiccups, by the way, was called Hubert.

'Boo?' said Hubert, looking puzzled. 'Hic. Nigel, why did you say boo?'

'Because,' said Nigel, 'giving people a good scare is the best way of curing hiccups.'

'Well, that was very kind of you, Nigel, hic,' said Hubert. 'But I'm not a people, I'm a dragon. And we dragons, as you know, are very hard to scare. Hic.'

'Blow into a paper bag!' cried his sister Cecily. 'That's the best cure for hiccups!'

'Oh?' said Hubert. 'Hic. Well, if you say so, Cecily.'

And he took a huge, deep, full, dragon's breath — and blew.

Bang! went the bag at once.

'Oh dear,' said Hubert, blushing. 'I think dragons are too blowy for paper bags, Cecily. Hic.'

'Water!' cried Aunt Florence. 'You have to drink from the far side of a glass of water! That's the best cure for hiccups!'

'Water?' said Hubert. 'Hic. That sounds like a good idea.'

And he reached for the water and lifted it to his mouth and drank from the far side of the glass, just as he was told.

Sizzle! went the water in Hubert's hot mouth.

'Oops,' said Hubert, lowering his eyes. 'I think dragons are too steamy for water, Aunt Florence. Hic.'

'Hold your breath!' cried Uncle Jaspar. 'Holding your breath for as long as you possibly can is the best cure for hiccups!'

'Really?' said Hubert. 'Hic. Well, all right, Uncle Jaspar, if you think that will work.'

And he took another huge, deep, full, dragon's breath —

And he held it and held it and held it and held it —

And he was still holding it when suddenly hot thick grey smoke began to pour from his ears.

Whooooooooooooooooooooooosh! went Hubert, letting go all his breath at once.

'No, no good,' he said, shuffling his feet. 'Dragons are too smoky for holding their breaths, Uncle Jaspar. Hic.'

'Stand on your head, Hubert!' cried everyone. 'When nothing else works, that's the best cure for hiccups!'

'Stand on my head?' said Hubert. 'Hic. How?'

'Don't worry, we'll help you!' cried everyone at once.

And Uncle Jaspar and Cecily took hold of Hubert's left hind leg.

And Aunt Florence and Nigel took hold of Hubert's right hind leg.

'Are you sure about this?' said Hubert, looking quite nervous. 'Hic.'

'Absolutely!' cried Uncle Jaspar. 'It's the best cure for hiccups, the very best there is! Everyone ready? Right! Up we go!'

And Uncle Jaspar and Cecily lifted Hubert's left hind leg —

And Aunt Florence and Nigel lifted Hubert's right hind leg —

And slowly, slowly, his huge, heavy, dragon's body trembling and shaking and swaying like a leaf, up went Hubert, up onto the very top of his head.

'Perfect!' cried Nigel.

'Wonderful!' cried Cecily.

'Terrific!' cried Aunt Florence.

'Hooray!' cried Uncle Jaspar.

'Hic,' said Hubert.

'What?' said everyone.

And whoops, before they could stop him, before they could hold him a second longer, down crashed Hubert, bang smash back to the floor.

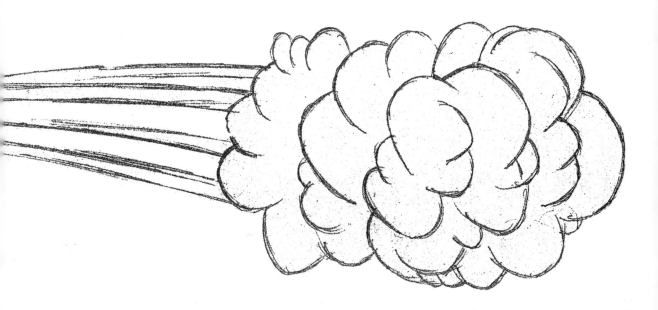

'Sorry, everyone,' said Hubert, blinking. 'I think dragons are too heavy for standing on their heads. Hic.'

'It's no use,' said Aunt Florence. 'Nothing is working. We'll just have to take him to the doctor.'

'The doctor?' said Hubert, his dragon eyes popping. 'Oh dear. Hic.'

Dr McIver was a small, fussy man with big, white, bushy eyebrows.

'We've tried absolutely everything,' everyone told him.

'Saying boo,' said Nigel.

'Blowing into a paper bag,' said Cecily.

'Drinking water from the far side of the glass,' said Aunt Florence.

'Holding your breath,' said Uncle Jaspar.

'They even made me stand on the very top of my head,' said Hubert. 'Hic.'

'Hiccups, hmm?' said Dr McIver. 'Well, you've come to the right place! Dr McIver's Super Special Anti-Hiccup Pills! Never fail!'

And he produced a huge jar filled to the brim with shiny green pills bigger than tennis balls and he took one out.

'Now, Hubert,' said Dr McIver, leaning close. 'Open wide and say *ahhh!*'

'Careful, Dr McIver!' cried Uncle Jaspar. 'You shouldn't —'

Too late, too late!

'Ahhh!' said Hubert.

And a mighty flame leapt from Hubert's mouth, the way flames do from dragons' mouths, in less than a second turning the good doctor's face as bright as a brick and sizzling his big, white, bushy eyebrows crispy black.

'Hold your fire, dragon!' cried Dr McIver. 'Hold your fire!'

'Oh dear!' cried Hubert, absolutely horrified. 'What have I done? I didn't mean it! Honestly! It just sort of popped out before I could even think!'

Dr McIver mopped his brow with an enormous white handkerchief.

'Phew!' he said. 'That was close!'

Dr McIver's face was a proper pink again, just the way it had been before, and his bushy eyebrows were all white again, too. Except for, well, maybe just the slightest smudge of black here and there.

'Oh, thank heavens!' cried Hubert. 'Thank heavens you're all right!'

'Look!' cried Uncle Jaspar. 'Hubert has stopped hiccupping!'

Hubert blinked his eyes.

'Why, so I have!' he said.

'Cured!' cried Dr McIver, clapping his hands. 'Another Dr McIver patient successfully cured!'

'Hooray!' cried everyone. 'Hooray!'

'Thank you, Dr McIver,' said Hubert, shaking the doctor's hand. 'Thank you very much.'

'My pleasure!' said Dr McIver. 'Any time! Now good-bye Hubert and home you go like a good dragon and have a good night's sleep.'

Night-Night!

The Talking Bow Tie

That evening Mr Baxter brought home a brand-new bow tie.

'Oh, very lovely!' said Mrs Baxter, and it was.

It was the boldest bright yellow with the biggest purple spots and it looked very happy and gay.

'I thought I'd wear it tonight,' said Mr Baxter.

Mr and Mrs Baxter were going out to dinner.

So Mr Baxter had a shower, and then he put on a nice clean white shirt (and his underwear and trousers and shoes and socks, too, of course), and then he popped himself in front of the big mirror in the bathroom and put on the brand-new bow tie.

'Oh, yes indeed!' he said, giving it a little straighten this way and that. 'Very smart!'

'Very smart?' said the bow tie.

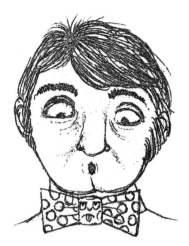

'What?' said Mr Baxter.

'You don't look very smart,' said the bow tie. 'You look ridiculous.'

'I beg your pardon?' said Mr Baxter.

'You are one of the most ridiculous-looking people I have ever seen,' said the bow tie.

'Mary!' cried Mr Baxter, running out of the bathroom. 'Mary! This bow tie just spoke to me! It said I looked ridiculous!'

Mrs Baxter was busy in the kitchen preparing dinner for the children, and she didn't really hear what Mr Baxter said.

'Well, wear something else, dear,' she said, serving up the children's lamb chops.

'What?' said Mr Baxter. 'Oh. All right.'

And he took off the bow tie and put on his favourite pale blue tie instead, which was very nice and had no spots at all.

16

The next morning when she was doing the clean-ing, Mrs Baxter saw the brand-new bow tie lying on the dressing table, where Mr Baxter had dropped it.

'Oh, how pretty!' she said, not remembering a single thing about it. She picked it up and held it to her hair. 'I think it suits me,' she said. 'Yes, I think I'll wear it this afternoon when I go shopping.'

'Your nose is too long,' said the bow tie.

'I beg your pardon?' said Mrs Baxter.

'It looks like a sausage,' said the bow tie. 'And your eyes are too small, too. They look like shrivelled raisins.'

'What?' said Mrs Baxter.

'In fact,' said the bow tie, 'your face is one of the silliest faces I have ever seen.'

'Oh, you horrid thing!' cried Mrs Baxter, and she flung the bow tie as far away as she could, out into the hall.

Now, the Baxters had two children, a boy and a girl. The boy's name was Michael. And at four o'clock that afternoon he came home, as usual, from school.

'Hi!' he called. 'Anyone home?'

There was a note on the kitchen table.

Gone to have my hair cut. Be back soon. There are some lovely new apples in the fruit bowl —

love Mother
XX

So Michael took an apple and started to munch it, and then he saw the brand-new bow tie lying on the floor in the hall.

'Hey, what a great bow tie!' he said, picking it up. 'I think I'll wear it to school tomorrow!'

'Don't be ridiculous,' said the bow tie.

'What?' said Michael. 'Who said that?'

'Your head's like a rubbish tin with the lid jammed on crooked,' said the bow tie.

'Get out of it!' said Michael.

'And the rest of you doesn't look too hot either, if you want to know the truth,' said the bow tie.

'I don't need this!' cried Michael, and he threw the bow tie down and went for a long, long ride on his bike.

Then Michael's sister came home. Her name was Suzie. She picked the bow tie up at once.

'Oh, how gorgeous!' she said.

'But you're not,' said the bow tie.

'Did you say something?' said Suzie.

'You've got a face like a pickled pillow,' said the bow tie. 'And your ears look like jug handles poking out of your head.'

'Well, I don't like you either,' said Suzie, and she threw the bow tie over her shoulder and went off to her room to read a good book.

Now, the Baxters had a dog, a very floppy and friendly dog, and his name was Ebenezer.

'I know,' said Mrs Baxter when she came home.

'I'll give that bow tie to Ebenezer. It wouldn't dare say anything to him.'

And she tied the bow tie very carefully around Ebenezer's neck.

'Yes,' she said. 'Quite nice.'

'What a smelly dog,' said the bow tie. 'He smells like an over-cooked cabbage. He smells like a pair of old socks.'

'Woof!' cried Ebenezer, and he tore off the bow tie and ran under the sofa in the front room and wouldn't come out all night.

The last member of the Baxter family to try the bow tie was the family cat. She was small and white and fluffy and her name was Daphne, and I don't quite know how she came to wear the bow tie, but she did.

'What a silly-looking cat,' said the bow tie. 'You look like a mouldy cheese. You look like a cross-eyed mop.'

'Meow!' cried Daphne, and she snatched off the bow tie and flew straight up the tallest tree in the garden and absolutely refused to come down, even for her supper.

'This has gone on quite long enough!' said Mr Baxter. 'That bow tie is totally terrible! It has insulted everyone! It must be taught a lesson at once! There is only one thing to do!'

And he put it in the refrigerator, in the freezer part, next to the fish fingers, and he left it there for three whole days and nights.

And when he took it out, believe you me, that talking bow tie never spoke again.

Night-Night!

The Frog Who Would Sing For The King

There was once a frog who loved to sing. His name was Bosphorous and he was a lovely green colour with big, bulgy eyes and he lived with all the other frogs in a large pond in a far corner of the kingdom. The pond was inky and murky and dark, though here and there dappled with sun, exactly the sort of pond that frogs love best.

25

'Tra la la,' sang Bosphorous, perched on a lily pad.

I sing the song of froggie swimming,
Backstroke,
Longstroke,
Downstroke,
Frogstroke,
Oh lovely, lovely, but nothing tops,
Doing froggie belly flops!

'Says who?' said the other frogs. 'Who says?'
'What?' said Bosphorous. 'I beg your pardon?'
'Singing is silly,' said the other frogs. 'Frogs don't sing. Frogs go gloop.'
'But I love to sing,' said Bosphorous. 'I have to sing. Singing is wonderful. Singing is life. And one day I shall sing for the King.'

'Sing for the King?' said the other frogs. 'Ha ha ha! Oh, don't make us laugh, Bosphorous! Gloop gloop!'

And into the inky dark waters of the pond they dived, leaving Bosphorous sitting on his lily pad all alone.

But Bosphorous sang on. His voice rang out rich and strong, as round as a pot, as warming as soup on a cold winter's day.

Tra la la, tra la la,
I sing the song of deep pond bottom,
Glurpy bubbles,
Inky weeds,
Slimy worms,
Oozy reeds,
Oh what heaven when you've got 'em,
For a froggie's muddy bottom!

'Gloop gloop!' went the other frogs. 'Silly Bosphorous! Gloop gloop!'

Now, across the hills and valleys on the other side
of the kingdom, all was far from well.

In the King's castle, there was a terrible scene.

'No, I can't eat this!' roared the King, hurling
away his supper, which was a lovely roast goose.
Splat! it went against the wall. 'I am much too
angry for food!'

The King was a little man with scarlet hair and a
scarlet face and his name was King Cedric and he
was always angry.

'But Your Majesty,' said the King's Advisor.
'You haven't eaten a single thing for days and days
and days.'

28

'Yar!' roared the King, his face becoming more scarlet than ever. 'Who cares? I am too angry to eat!'

And he hurled away his salt and pepper too — bang! bang! — against the wall.

'May I advise some music, Sire?' said the King's Advisor, who was tall and lean with grindy fingers and a long, crafty nose.

'Music?' roared the King. 'What music? How can you speak of music at a time like this?'

'Because music will distract you from your cares and woes,' said the King's Advisor, tapping his crafty nose. 'And you will eat your supper and feel soothed and all will be well in the kingdom.'

And he snapped his fingers and into the King's chamber strode three tall trumpeteers.

Blare blare! they shrilled. *Blare blare!*

'Out!' roared the King at once. 'Out! Oh, what a dreadful noise! I feel even angrier than ever!'

'A thousand pardons, Sire,' said the King's Advisor, bowing to the floor. 'My deepest apologies. Not the kind of music I intended for Your Majesty at all. But if you will allow me, Sire.'

And again he snapped his fingers, and this time into the King's chamber came three small men carrying violins.

Screech screech! went the violins. *Screech screech!*

'Out!' roared the King. 'Out!'

The King was so angry this time that his face leapt from scarlet to royal purple.

'Oh, they were even more horrible than the ones before!' he cried. 'Out! Out! And you, too!' he roared at his Advisor. 'And if you can't find me the right kind of music, then you needn't bother ever coming back!'

'Yes, Sire,' said the King's Advisor, scurrying backwards from the King's chamber. 'Yes, Sire,' bowing so low his long nose scraped the floor.

For three weeks, day and night, the King's Advisor rode about the kingdom, searching for the music to soothe his angry King. And in one village he heard the music of flutes, and in another of harps, and in a third of drums. But the drums were too noisy, and the harps were too sleepy, and the flutes were too sad.

'No,' said the King's Advisor, grinding his fingers. 'That's not the music I need for my King.'

And he had almost given up when one day he found himself by a pond. The King's Advisor was tired. He thought he would rest a while. He dismounted from his horse and sat down on the grass by the inky dark waters of the pond.

'Gloop gloop,' he heard all around. 'Gloop gloop.'

'Frogs,' said the King's Advisor. 'This pond must be full of frogs.'

And then suddenly he heard something else.

'Tra la la!' he heard. 'Tra la la!'

It was the song of Bosphorous, rich and strong, as round as a pot, as warming as soup.

'That's it!' cried the King's Advisor, leaping to his feet. 'That's the music I've been searching for! That's exactly it!'

In his castle, King Cedric was as angry as ever.

'Yar!' he cried, hurling away yet another dinner, six splendid roast quails this time. Splot! they went against the wall.

The King's Advisor tiptoed into the King's chamber bearing Bosphorous the frog.

'Yar!' shouted the King. 'Who is it? What do you want?'

'Sing,' whispered the King's Advisor to Bosphorous. 'Sing, Bosphorous, sing!'

'Tra la la!' sang Bosphorous. 'Tra la la!'

I sing the song of insect pudding,
Waterbug noses,
Mosquito wings,
Tiny gnat knees,
And suchlike things,
Yum yum, yum yum,
In my froggie's tum!

'Bring me lamb chops!' cried King Cedric. 'Bring me porridge! Bring me bananas and carrots and chocolates and stew! I am cured of my anger! I am hungry at last!'

And he commanded Bosphorous to sit beside him, on a special red velvet cushion, by the King's right hand.

'My dear Bosphorous,' said King Cedric, 'you have made me well with your joyous song and to-morrow I shall bestow upon you the highest honour in the land. A royal banquet, filled with music and song!'

'Tra la la!' sang Bosphorous, bulging with happiness, as only a frog can bulge. 'Tra la la!'

I sing the song of frogs and kings,
Golden goblets,
Shining trumpets,
Snapping banners,
Toasted crumpets,
Hooray for the King, exceedingly fond,
And me beside him, the whole world our pond!

Night-Night!

Tiny Timothy

Timothy was a little boy. In fact, he was tiny. He was very small. He was going to be six on his next birthday — he was practically six already! — and he would certainly grow lots and lots when he got to be six, but meanwhile he was still very small.

And because he was so very small, all sorts of nasty people did all sorts of nasty things to him.

They bossed him.

They bullied him.

They blamed him.

They pushed him and pulled him and picked on him and gave him a terrible time.

'Stop talking, Timothy!' shouted Miss Fairfax, Timothy's teacher at school.

Miss Fairfax had a nose like a purple beetroot and her hair looked like a worn-out kitchen mop.

'But I wasn't talking, Miss Fairfax,' said Timothy.

'Oh, don't you dare answer me back, you horrid little child!' screeched Miss Fairfax. And she became at once so angry that the rest of her face turned the colour of a beetroot, too. 'Go and stand in the corner!' she screeched. 'And you can stay there until you've counted to a thousand! Backwards!'

And poor little Timothy had to do it, too.

'Clean up your room!' snapped Timothy's Aunt Mildred. 'I've never seen such a terrible mess! Clean it up at once!'

Aunt Mildred lived in the house and looked after Timothy while his mother was out at work. She was long and bony and her face was blue and she was always shivering and always felt cold.

'But I made it all neat this morning, Aunt Mildred,' said Timothy. 'And I haven't been in there all day.'

'Do as you're told at once, you stupid little thing!'
shouted Aunt Mildred, her icy eyes glaring and her
blue face becoming even more blue. 'Or I'll send
you to bed without any supper at all!'

And poor little Timothy had to clean up all by
himself the terrible mess his big sister Stephanie had
made.

'Stop dawdling!' shouted Mrs Sims.

Mrs Sims was the lollipop lady who crossed all
the children over the road at school. She was heavy
and red and round and puffy and she was always
blowing her whistle and waving her arms and shouting at everyone to hurry up.

'But I wasn't dawdling, Mrs Sims,' said Timothy.
'I was walking as fast as I could.'

'Oh, I'm reporting you to the headmaster, you
beastly little creature!' cried Mrs Sims. And she

puffed up even more until she looked like she was going to absolutely explode. 'You'll soon see what you get for dawdling!' she cried.

And poor little Timothy had to stay back after school all by himself for a whole hour, kept in for dawdling he hadn't even done.

Poor little Timothy.

Except he wasn't really so poor.

Because under his pillow in bed at home Timothy had the most wonderful secret thing.

A tiny invisible bottle filled to the top with tiny invisible magic pills.

'Right!' said Timothy in the dark, all snug in his bed.

And he reached under his pillow for the invisible bottle and carefully, carefully he unscrewed the top.

Carefully, carefully Timothy poured out three invisible magic pills.

And then he swallowed them, one after the other.

Swallow.

Swallow.

Swallow.

He closed his eyes.

'Miss Fairfax!' he whispered.

And just like that Timothy turned into the biggest, hairiest, most ferocious-looking gorilla.

'Now!' he growled.

And in a flash he was out of bed and swinging through the night, straight to Miss Fairfax's house.

Miss Fairfax was sitting in her front room, scowling at a newspaper.

Timothy the gorilla tapped on her window.

'Yes?' she said, looking up.

And when she saw the big, hairy, ferocious gorilla staring at her through the window, Miss Fairfax turned as white as a sheet — even her purple beetroot nose turned white! — and she fainted dead away.

'Ha ha,' chuckled Timothy, swinging away into the night.

The next night Timothy did it again.

Swallow.

Swallow.

Swallow.

'Aunt Mildred!' he whispered.

And just like that Timothy became the biggest, whitest, most powerful polar bear.

Aunt Mildred was in the kitchen, shivering over a cup of tea.

Timothy the polar bear padded in on all fours and stood quietly beside her chair.

'Who's that?' said Aunt Mildred, looking up with a shiver.

And when she saw the big, white, powerful polar bear standing right there beside her, Aunt Mildred gave her most enormous shiver ever and turned even whiter than the polar bear and fainted dead away.

'Ha ha,' chuckled Timothy, padding off silently into the night.

And now it was time for Mrs Sims.

Timothy reached under his pillow for the tiny invisible bottle.

What sort of animal would he become tonight?

Swallow.

Swallow.

Swallow.

'Mrs Sims!' he whispered.

And already he could feel himself starting to roar.

Night-Night!

The Elephant On The Doorstep

One day the mother opened the front door and there on the doorstep stood an elephant.

A real elephant.

And a nice-sized one, too.

Not too enormously huge.

But not too tiny either.

'Oh, can we keep him?' cried the little girl. 'Please, Mummy, please, please, please?'

'Oh, yes, Mummy!' cried the little boy. 'We can ride him to school and have games and races and do all sorts of wonderful things! Oh, let's, let's! I've always wanted an elephant!'

The elephant on the doorstep blinked his big, soft eyes up and down three times and then gave his trunk a little wave.

'Oh, look, Mummy!' cried the little girl and boy both together. 'He likes us! He wants to come in!'

The mother laughed.

'Children, children!' she said, 'We can't have an elephant in the family just like that. I mean, elephants don't just appear on doorsteps. I'm sure he belongs to someone and has just got himself a little lost.'

The little boy frowned.

'You mean, he's escaped from the zoo?' he said, and he looked at once quite sad.

'Or the circus?' said the little girl, and she looked sad, too.

Just then the father appeared. He had been reading his newspaper and his special reading glasses were still perched on the very end of his nose.

'Elephants?' he said, blinking. 'What's all this about elephants?'

And then he saw the elephant standing on the doorstep.

'Help!' he cried. 'An elephant! A real elephant! Quick, close the door, someone, before he jumps in!'

'Relax, dear, relax,' said the mother, putting her hand gently on the father's arm. 'He's not doing anything wrong. Actually,' she said, laughing again, 'he's one of the best-behaved elephants I've ever seen.'

The elephant on the doorstep gave another little wave of his trunk.

'Well, I don't want him in the house,' the father said, 'treading all over the carpets and knocking over all the vases and disturbing all the books!'

And he rattled his newspaper, to show how serious he was.

'He's escaped from the zoo,' said the little boy.

'Or the circus,' said the little girl.

'Yes,' said the mother. 'Let me phone them now and see if we can find out exactly where he belongs.'

The mother picked up the telephone in the hall.

'Hello,' she said to the man at the zoo. 'Are you missing an elephant by any chance?'

'Just a minute,' said the man, and they heard him

counting. 'One, two, three, four, five, six, seven, eight,' he counted. 'No,' he said to the mother. 'All our elephants seem to be here.'

'Thank you,' said the mother. Next she dialled the circus. 'Hello,' she said. 'You haven't lost an elephant, have you?'

'Hmm, let me look,' said the circus man, and again they heard the sound of counting. 'One, two, three, four, five, six,' they heard. 'No,' said the circus man. 'We haven't lost any elephants today.'

'Thank you,' said the mother.

'Oh, can we keep him, can we keep him?' the little girl and boy cried, clapping their hands and

jumping up and down. 'Oh, let's, let's, please, please!'

The mother thought for a moment.

'Well,' she said at last. 'I think this is the best thing. Let's put a notice in the window at the corner shop, so that if someone has lost him, they'll know where he is. Meanwhile, he can stay with us. We'll put him in the garden.'

'The garden?' cried the father. 'But he'll sit in all the deck chairs!'

'Daddy,' said the little girl. 'Elephants don't sit in deck chairs.'

'He'll fiddle with the barbecue!' cried the father.

'Daddy,' said the little boy. 'Elephants don't fiddle with barbecues.'

'Well,' said the father, rattling his newspaper, 'I'm sure he'll do *something*!'

'Relax, dear,' said the mother, laughing. 'It'll be perfectly all right.'

'I think he's hungry,' said the little girl, when they'd taken the elephant round to the garden.

'I think he's thirsty,' said the little boy.

And the elephant must have been, because look at what he ate for his supper:

He ate sixty-seven sticky buns.

And he drank forty-two bottles of milk.

And then he had thirty-six crisp, bright, shiny red apples for afters.

And then he went to sleep on a big pile of old blankets in a warm corner of the garage.

'Night-night, elephant!' said the little girl.

'Night-night, elephant!' said the little boy.

And then it was time for the little girl and boy to go to bed, too.

'Night-night, children,' said the mother and father, giving them a kiss and tucking them in.

The little girl and boy lay wide awake in their beds. They were too excited to sleep.

'Oh, I hope no one comes to get him,' said the little girl.

'So do I,' said the little boy.

'It's wonderful having your own elephant.'

'It's better than anything.'

'I think we should call him Sam,' said the little girl.

'Or Harold,' said the little boy.

'Oh, I can't wait till tomorrow,' they both said together. 'I can't wait to see our elephant again!'

Night-Night!

Rosie On The Swing

This is about Rosie.

Rosie was a little girl whose favourite word was 'More!'

Whatever you gave her, that's what she always said.

If you gave her an ice-cream, say —

Or a lovely banana —

Or a big ripe peach —

Before she had even eaten it —

Or sometimes even started —

'More!' Rosie would cry. 'More!'

If you gave her a new pair of soft pink socks —
Or a colouring book with fifty colour pencils —
Or took her swimming all day at the beach —
'More!' Rosie would cry. 'More! More!'

Sometimes you thought it was the only word Rosie could say.

Oh, she was really quite dreadful.

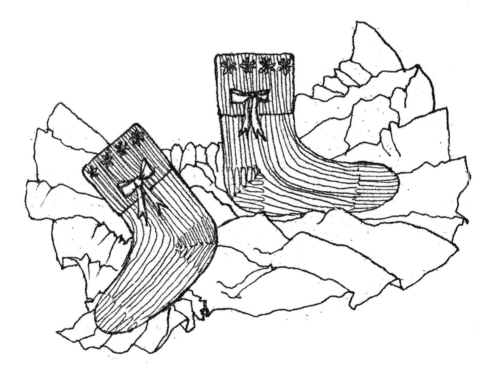

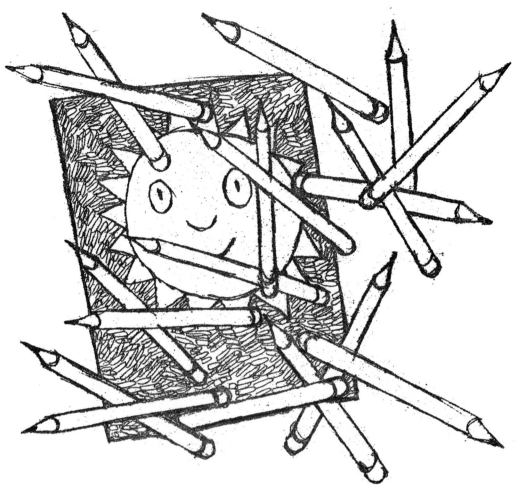

One day Rosie's father took Rosie to the park.

It was a splendid day, too, all light and bright and sunny, with just the softest breeze moving the leaves on the trees all around.

'Now,' said Rosie's father. 'What about a nice swing?'

Rosie, by the way, had the biggest blue eyes and the reddest rosy cheeks and the cutest little nose and the longest blonde hair that fell straight down her back to her waist.

Oh, she was really quite pretty.

Except, of course, when she was shouting, 'More!'

Rosie's father lifted Rosie carefully onto the swing and first he made sure she was holding on properly and then he gave her a little push, very gently, just to get her started.

'More!' cried Rosie at once. 'More!'

'More?' said Rosie's father.

Now, Rosie's father was a terribly kind man who always tried to give his daughter whatever she wanted, and so he gave Rosie a second push, just a teeny bit harder this time than the first.

'More!' cried Rosie. 'More! More!'

Well, in almost no time at all, that swing was absolutely *flying*! I mean, it was zooming so high that each time at the top it was almost out of sight.

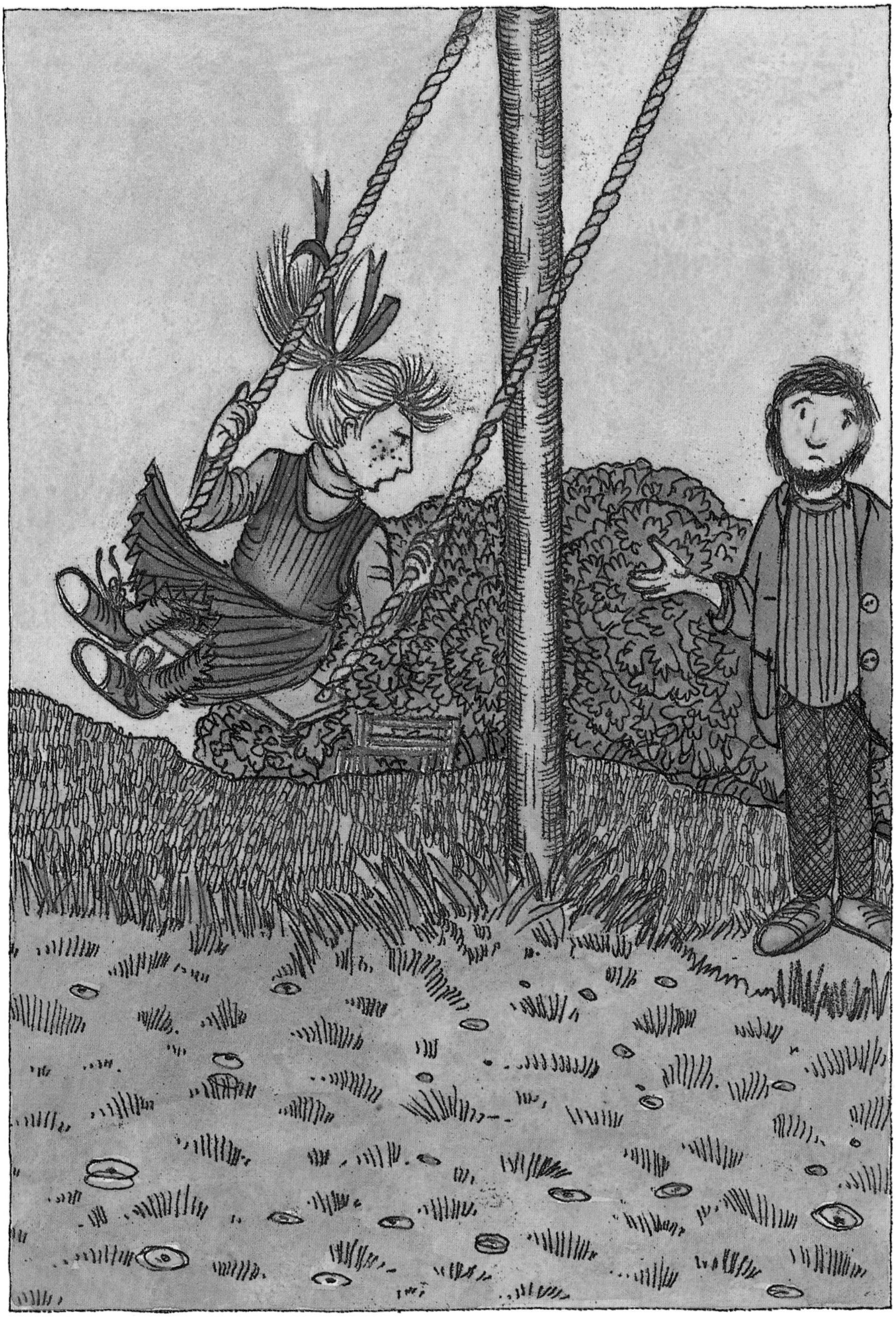

While Rosie's father, I have to tell you, was pushing so hard that his face looked just like a giant tomato.

Worse.

It looked like it was going to explode.

And still that dreadful child screamed, 'More! More! More!'

Up flew the swing, up and up, higher and higher.

And then suddenly this happened.

Just like that, without the slightest warning, that beastly Rosie shot off the swing and sailed through the air and landed — plop! — right on the very top of the very tallest tree in the whole park.

Rosie's father was horrified.

His mouth fell completely open.

His eyes practically popped right out of his head.

'Good heavens!' he cried. 'Rosie!'

And, not wasting another single second, Rosie's father ran as fast as he could to the fire station, which was luckily just around the corner, and in less than a minute back he raced with a bright red fire engine filled with firemen and the longest ladder on top.

Up shot the ladder, up against the tree.

'No, no!' cried Rosie's father to the firemen. 'Rosie is my daughter! I'll do it!'

And up the ladder he went.

Now, Rosie's father didn't like going up ladders. Ladders scared him. Ladders frightened him. Ladders made him feel giddy and wonky and wobbly all over, as shaky as a jelly from head to toe.

And this was the longest ladder Rosie's father had ever had to go up in his whole life.

In fact, it was so long that at the very top it was actually swaying, this way and that way, to and fro in the breeze.

Rosie's father's hands trembled and shook. His knees knocked together like two coconuts. His heart thumped and bumped like a runaway drum.

But Rosie's father didn't think about that. All he could think about was Rosie.

'Oh, my poor little girl!' he thought, as he climbed and climbed. 'What a terrible thing to happen! How frightened she must be!'

Whoops!

Rosie's father was suddenly at the top, the very top of the ladder.

He looked quickly across.

And yes, there was Rosie, with her big blue eyes and her red rosy cheeks and her cute little nose and her long blonde hair, perched on top of the tree.

And look!

Not only was Rosie perched up there, but a pigeon was perched there, too, come to roost right on top of Rosie's head, and the pigeon was making that special soft warbly sound that only pigeons can make:

Corrrrrrrrrr corrrrrrrrrrr.

Rosie's father reached across with trembling hands to lift his darling daughter to safety.

And what Rosie said, of course, was 'More!'

'I beg your pardon?' said Rosie's father.

'More!' cried Rosie. 'More! More!'

Rosie's father stared hard at his shouting daughter.

'No, I don't think so,' he said firmly. 'I think you have had quite enough for one day, my dear.'

'Oh?' said Rosie, blinking her big eyes.

'I think it's time you had your supper,' he said. 'I think it's time you went to bed. Unless, that is, you'd like to stay up in this tree all night.'

'Oh, no!' said Rosie quickly. 'I've had enough, thank you, Daddy! I've had more than enough!'

'Good,' said Rosie's father. 'There's a good girl.'

And Rosie's father lifted Rosie off the tree and down the ladder together they went, and then hand in hand, just as it was getting dark, too, all the way home.

Night-Night!

The Little Girl Who Did Not Believe In Witches

There was once a little girl who did not believe in witches.

'Witches are silly,' she said. 'Anyhow, there aren't even any such things.'

The little girl's name was Maizie and she lived with her mother in quite a nice house.

One afternoon there was a knock on the door.

Maizie opened it at once.

There on the doorstep stood a strange-looking woman.

A very strange-looking woman indeed.

She looked, in fact, just like a witch.

She was dressed completely in black, just like a witch.

She wore a long, pointy, black hat, just like a witch.

And a long, black cloak that reached right down to the ground, just like a witch.

And a pair of long, black, pointy shoes poking out underneath, just like a witch always wears.

Her nose was long and pointy, too, the way witches' noses always are, and so was her chin.

'Goodness!' said Maizie to herself. 'She looks just like a witch! Except I don't believe in witches, of course, because there aren't any such things!'

'Oh, excuse me, little girl,' said the strange-looking woman. 'May I use your telephone? There seems to be something wrong with my broom.'

It was a tall broom made out of twigs all tied together in a bunch on a long wooden handle. Just exactly the sort of broom that witches always have.

'Certainly!' said Maizie, who did not believe in witches, of course, and was very polite, too. 'It's right here.'

And she pointed to the telephone in the hall.

'Hello, Francesca?' said the woman into the telephone. 'Hazel here. There seems to be something wrong with my broom. Could you come and have a look at it for me? I'll tell you where I am.'

And she did.

'There!' she said to Maizie. 'Shouldn't be long. Francesca is quick as lightning, usually.'

In fact, she was even quicker.

Before Maizie could blink, there stood Francesca on the doorstep.

And what a strange-looking woman she was, too.

Francesca was dressed completely in black, with a black, pointy hat, and a long, black cloak, and long, black, pointy shoes poking out underneath.

'Goodness!' said Maizie to herself. 'She looks just like a witch, too! Except I don't believe in witches, of course, because there aren't any such things!'

'Hello, little girl,' said Francesca. 'May I come in?'

'Certainly!' said Maizie. 'We're just here in the hall.'

Francesca stepped inside.

'Well!' she said to Hazel. 'Let's see that broom of yours. Ah, here's the trouble!'

And she gave the handle of Hazel's broom a little twist.

'There we are!' she said. 'Right as rain again!

They get a bit stiff sometimes,' she said to Maizie. 'Well, good-bye!'

And as quickly as she had appeared, Francesca was gone.

'I don't believe in witches!' said Maizie to herself. 'Witches are silly! They don't even exist!'

'Well, little girl,' said Hazel. 'That was very kind of you to let me use your telephone. Thank you very much. Would you like a ride on my broom?'

'My mother will be home soon,' said Maizie. 'She works in a shop.'

'Oh, we won't be late,' said Hazel. 'Now hold on tight! Here we go!'

'I don't believe in witches!' said Maizie to herself as the broom zoomed high into the sky. 'This is not really happening. This is just a trick.'

Over the chimneys they soared, over the rooftops, over all the houses, over all the trees.

'I don't believe this,' said Maizie. 'This is not real.'

Three times round the sky they went, in huge, huge circles, round and round.

'It's only a trick,' said Maizie. 'It's not really happening at all.'

And then down they came again, right at Maizie's front door.

'Good-bye now, little girl,' said Hazel.

And with a wave, she was gone.

Then Maizie's mother came home from work.

'Hello, dear,' she said, giving Maizie a hug and a kiss. 'Have a nice day?'

'I don't believe in witches!' said Maizie. 'Witches are silly! They don't even exist!'

'Of course they don't,' said her mother. 'Witches are just made up.'

But that night, after her bath, Maizie went to the broom cupboard.

'Well, come on!' she shouted at the household broom. 'Don't just stand there! Do something!'

But the household broom, of course, which was just an ordinary broom, didn't do anything.

'Hmmm,' said Maizie, staring at it. 'Well, all right!' she said finally. 'I'll give you another chance tomorrow!'

In bed that night, and the next night, too, and the night after — in fact, every single night for weeks and weeks and weeks — Maizie thought about how she had flown on that special broomstick over the chimneys and rooftops and houses and trees, of how she had flown in those huge, huge circles, round and round, three times around the sky.

And of course she still didn't believe in witches, because witches were silly and they didn't even exist.

'Except,' said Maizie to herself, as she slipped off to sleep, 'except for, well, maybe just now and then.'

Night-Night!

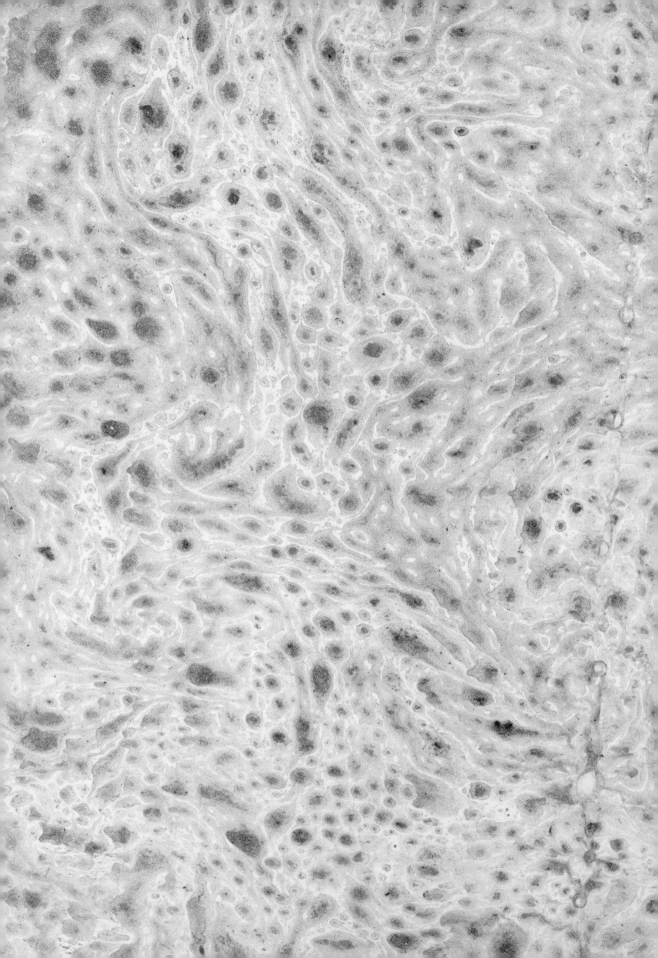